To Toshi and Jaxson

For information address Hyperion Books for Children, 125 West End Avenue, New York, New York 10023.
Printed in Malaysia
Reinforced binding
First Edition, January 2010
10 9 8
FAC-029191-16281

Library of Congress Cataloging-in-Publication Data on file.
ISBN: 978-1-4231-1990-6

Visit www.hyperionbooksforchildren.com and www.pigeonpresents.com

I Am Going!

By Mo Willems

An ELEPHANT & PIGGIE Book

Hyperion Books for Children/*New York*
AN IMPRINT OF DISNEY BOOK GROUP

This is a good day.

Just like yesterday.

Yes!

Yesterday was
a good day, too.

Well, I am going.

You are *going*?!

You are going away?!

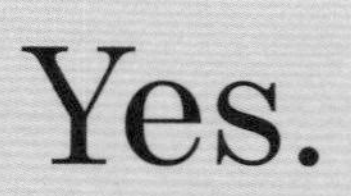
Yes.

You cannot go!

You must not go!

I WILL NOT
LET YOU GO!!!

POP!

I am going.

PIG

GIE!

What about me?

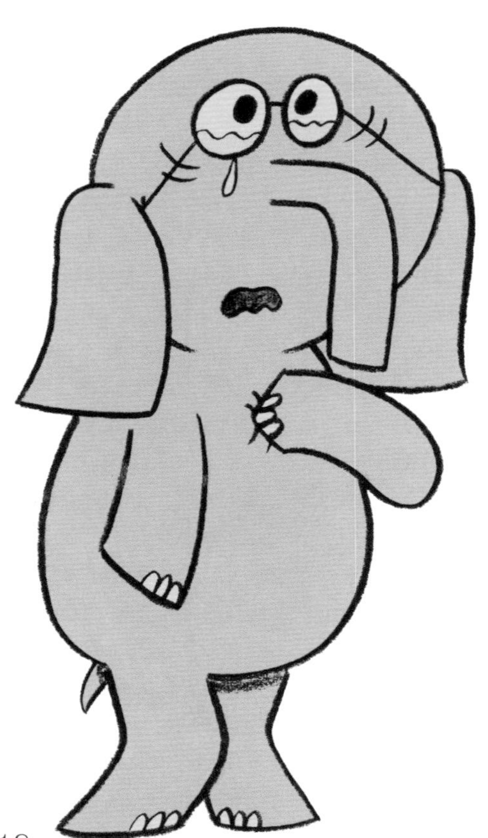

Who will I
skip with?

Who will I play
Ping-Pong with?

Who will I wear
a silly hat with?

WHO WILL I
SKIP AND
PLAY PING-PONG
IN A SILLY HAT
WITH?!?!

I am sorry,
Gerald.

But, I am going.

Fine.

Then *I* will
go, too!

Watch me go!

I am going!

Look at me go!

Have fun.

WAIT!

Go later!

Go tomorrow!

Go next week!

Go next month!

GO NEXT YEAR!!!

I am
going now.

NOW!?!

Why,
Piggie?

Why? Why?

Why? Why?

Why? Why?

Why?

Why?

Why?

Why?

Why?

Why?

Why?
Why?
Why?
Why?
Why?
Why?
Why?
Why?
Why?

Why?
Why?
Why?
Why?
Why?
Why?
Why?
Why
Why

Why?

It is lunchtime, Gerald.

Lunchtime?

I am going to
eat lunch.

You are going to eat lunch?
Yes.

Oh.

Piggie?

Yes,
Gerald?

Is it a
big lunch?

This is a good day.

Just like yesterday...

Have you read all of Elephant and Piggie's funny adventures?

Today I Will Fly!
My Friend Is Sad
I Am Invited to a Party!
There Is a Bird on Your Head!
(Theodor Seuss Geisel Medal)
I Love My New Toy!
I Will Surprise My Friend!
Are You Ready to Play Outside?
(Theodor Seuss Geisel Medal)
Watch Me Throw the Ball!
Elephants Cannot Dance!
Pigs Make Me Sneeze!
I Am Going!
Can I Play Too?
We Are in a Book!
(Theodor Seuss Geisel Honor)
I Broke My Trunk!
(Theodor Seuss Geisel Honor)
Should I Share My Ice Cream?
Happy Pig Day!
Listen to My Trumpet!
Let's Go for a Drive!
(Theodor Seuss Geisel Honor)
A Big Guy Took My Ball!
(Theodor Seuss Geisel Honor)
I'm a Frog!
My New Friend Is So Fun!
Waiting Is Not Easy!
(Theodor Seuss Geisel Honor)
I Will Take a Nap!
I *Really* Like Slop!
The Thank You Book